Stories From Our Street

Written by Richard Tulloch
Illustrated by Julie Vivas

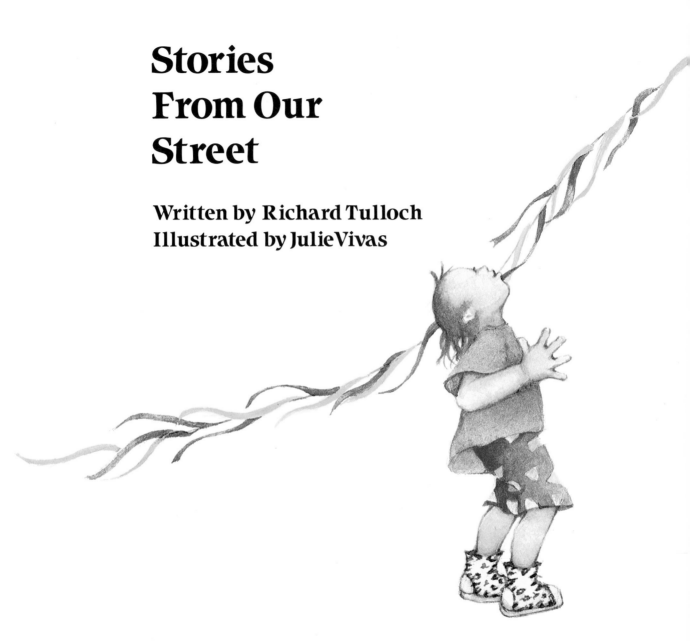

Kids Can Press Ltd.
TORONTO

The Catching Tree

At the end of our street there's a park with a big tree.
It's a Catching Tree, that catches things.

We went to the park with a blue and yellow kite.
It dipped and it flipped at the end of its string,
round and round and up and down.

But the Catching Tree caught it.

We tried everything but we couldn't get it down.

We played in the park with a red rubber ball.
We bounced it on the path, we rolled it down the hill
and we threw the ball as high as we could . . .

And the Catching Tree caught it.

We tried everything but we couldn't get it down.

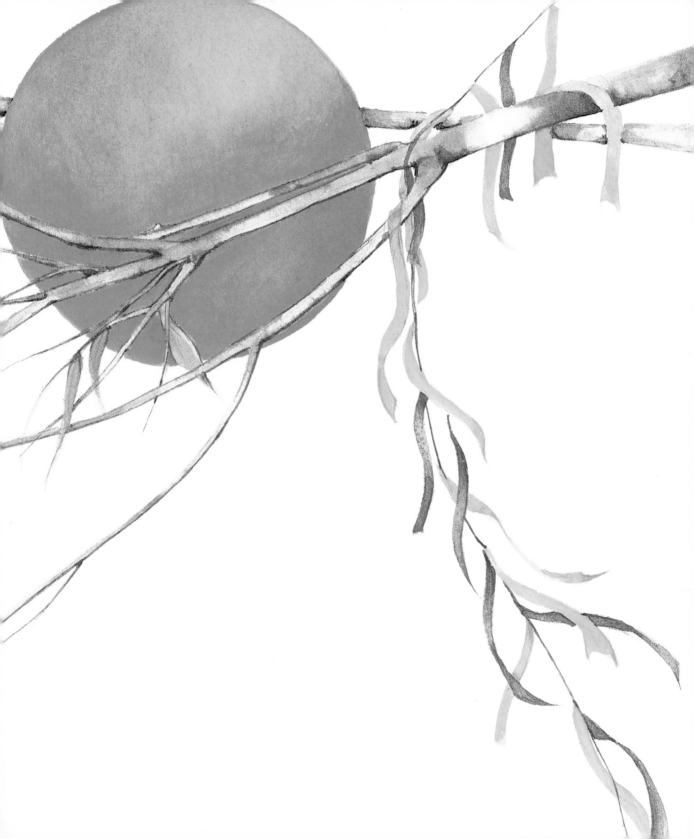

We played in the park with a shiny green aeroplane.
We wound up the propellor and let it go.

The aeroplane whirred and purred, looped the loop,
under and over, higher and higher and higher . . .

Then the Catching Tree caught it.

We tried everything but
we couldn't get it down.

So we went back to the park
with a long silver ladder.
Mum climbed up and shook
the Catching Tree as hard
as she could.
And down came the
blue and yellow kite.

She poked the Catching Tree
with the end of a broom.
And down came the red rubber ball.

She climbed to the top of
the ladder and reached up
as high as she could . . .

CRACK! Down came the ladder.

And the Catching Tree caught our Mum.
We tried everything, but we couldn't get her down.

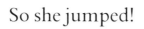

So she jumped!

Bored

It's raining outside in our street and we're bored.
There's nothing to do in our house, nothing at all.

Our baby's asleep so we can't make a noise.
We've read all our books and played all our games and
we're tired of our toys and there's nothing to watch
on TV, only talking and golf.

We're really, really bored.

Just a minute. The rain's stopping.
We can play outside!

But there's no-one to play with outside and we're bored.
There's nothing to do in our street, nothing at all.

The dog next door can't come out and play.
The lady next door says that if he goes out
he'll splash in the puddles and roll in the mud and
then come in and ruin her carpet.

We are really, really, really bored.

Just a minute. I know. We can go down to the park!

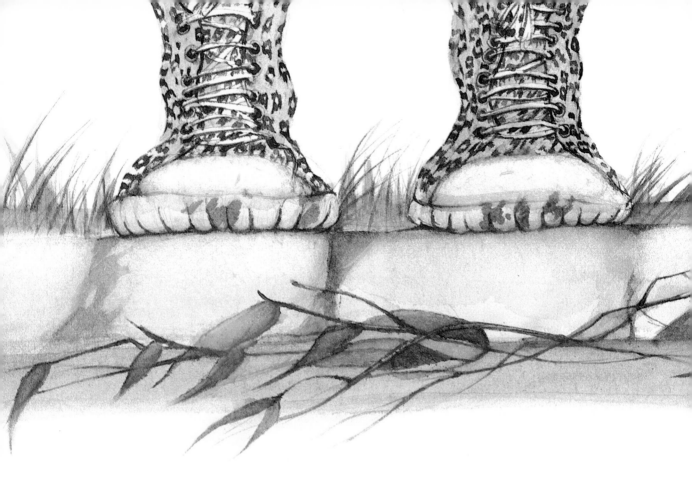

But the grass is all wet in the park and we're bored.
There's nothing to do in the park, nothing at all.

We are really, really, really, really . . .

Just a minute . . . look!

In the water in the gutter there's a little piece
of stick, and hanging on the stick there's a small
black beetle. He'll play with us.

We can pull him out and dry him and make a house for him. A special beetle house, with leaves for him to eat, and holes to let the air in so our beetle friend can breathe.

And when it's getting dark, and Mum comes out to call,
'Time to come in!', we call back, 'In a minute, Mum.'

'Cause we are really, really, really, really, really, really busy.

Wet Paint

One day Mr Murphy from a house down our street painted his front fence.

First he painted it pink and then he painted it green – smooth and shiny, gleaming wet green.

Mr Murphy was very proud of his new green fence.
He admired it for a long time and then went inside
to clean his brushes.

And while he was gone . . .

A bird flew down and landed on the wet green fence.
It walked along the top, leaving a line of pointy
pink footmarks.

Mr Murphy came running with his face all red.

'Shoo! Scram! That paint's still wet!
Go away, bird, and leave my fence alone!'

The bird flew up and landed on the top of Mr Murphy's
house, leaving a line of pointy green footmarks
across his roof.

Mr Murphy was cross.
He painted over the pointy pink footmarks on the
smooth and shiny, gleaming wet green fence.
And before he went inside he put up a sign
'WET PAINT!'

But while he was gone . . .

The dog next door came and sniffed the wet green fence.
A big blob of green stuck to the end of his nose.
A big patch of pink showed through the green on
Mr Murphy's fence.

Mr Murphy came running with his face all red,
waving his arms.

'Shoo! Scram! That paint's still wet!
Go away, dog, and leave my fence alone!'

The dog next door ran around barking.
He stepped in a puddle of paint and left sticky green
paw-marks all over Mr Murphy's path.

Mr Murphy was very cross. He painted over the pink
patch on the smooth and shiny, gleaming wet green fence.
And before he went inside he put up a new sign
'WET PAINT. DO NOT TOUCH.'

But while he was gone . . .

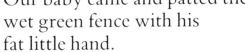

Our baby came and patted the
wet green fence with his
fat little hand.

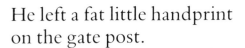

He left a fat little handprint
on the gate post.

He put his hand on his head
and got sticky green paint
in his hair. Yuk!

Mr Murphy came running
with his face all red,
waving his arms and
shaking his fists and
shouting at our baby
at the top of his voice.

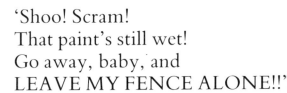

'Shoo! Scram!
That paint's still wet!
Go away, baby, and
LEAVE MY FENCE ALONE!!'

Our baby started to cry.

Mr Murphy picked him up and brought him back
to our house. 'There, there,' he said,
'I didn't really mean it.'

Our baby shoved his sticky green hand right in
Mr Murphy's face. Yuk!

Mr Murphy was very, very cross. He washed his face and
painted over our baby's handprint on the smooth and
shiny, gleaming wet green fence. He put up another new sign
'WET PAINT. DO NOT TOUCH. THIS MEANS YOU!'

The next morning I got up very early. I went down
the street and looked at Mr Murphy's smooth and
shiny, gleaming wet green fence.

I looked at the sign
'WET PAINT. DO NOT TOUCH. THIS MEANS YOU!'

I reached out my hand and with the tip of my
finger I touched the smooth and shiny, gleaming
wet green paint.

But Mr Murphy didn't come running with his face all red.

His new green fence was dry.

To Agnes

Printed by permission of Cambridge University Press, England.

First Canadian edition published 1989

Canadian Cataloguing in Publication Data

Tulloch, Richard
    Stories from our street

ISBN 0-921103-62-X

I. Vivas, Julie, 1947–   . II. Title.

PZ7.T843Sto 1989   j823'.914   C89-093406-1

Kids Can Press Ltd.
585 1/2 Bloor Street West
Toronto, Ontario, Canada M6G 1K5

Printed and bound in Hong Kong by Wing King Tong

89 0 9 8 7 6 5 4 3 2 1